BULLDOZER GOES TO SCHOOL

BULLDOZER AND FRIENDS

BULLDOZER GOES TO SCHOOL

Elise Broach

Illustrated by
Kelly Murphy

Christy Ottaviano Books
LITTLE, BROWN AND COMPANY
New York   Boston

ALSO BY ELISE BROACH AND KELLY MURPHY

BULLDOZER AND FRIENDS

Bulldozer's Big Rescue

THE MASTERPIECE ADVENTURES

The Miniature World of Marvin & James

James to the Rescue

Trouble at School for Marvin & James

Marvin & James Save the Day (and Elaine Helps!)

A Trip to the Country for Marvin & James

For my wonderful cousin Laura Broach—
great teacher, great reader, great friend
—EB

For Alanna, whose kindness is helping
teach the next generation
—KM

BULLDOZER GOES TO SCHOOL

Contents

CHAPTER 1
First Day 1

CHAPTER 2
Too Many People 21

CHAPTER 3
Trouble at Circle Time 45

CHAPTER 4
The Playground 65

CHAPTER 5
Cleaning Up 89

Word Play 105

CHAPTER 1
First Day

Bulldozer is nervous. It is the first day of school, and he has never been to this school before. What if he makes a mistake? What if the other kids laugh at him? What if he doesn't like it?

So many things to worry about!

Bulldozer's mother tells him it will all be fine.

"Anything new is scary the first time," she says. "But you'll like this school, B! You'll make new friends, and you'll get even better at math and reading. You'll learn so many things."

"I already know math," Bulldozer says. "Forty-nine plus one is forty-ten."

"Try fifty," his mother says.

"I know how to read, too," Bulldozer tells her. He takes out his favorite book and reads the story very quickly.

"There was a train. It couldn't go up the hill. It tried and tried. And then it did!" He looks at his mother. "See?"

"That's great," his mother says. "But this year at school you will learn how to read even better."

"I don't think I need school," Bulldozer says. "I would rather stay here and build a clubhouse."

"You can do that after school," his mother says.

Bulldozer doesn't like this idea.

"Maybe I can go to school a different day," he says. "Tomorrow."

"You can go to school tomorrow," his mother says. "But you are also going today."

The way his mother talks, Bulldozer knows it is hopeless. He will have to go to school.

The new school is a big brick building five blocks from his house. It has tall windows and a long parking lot, and there are fields and woods behind it. Bulldozer went there once during the summer to visit his classroom and meet his new teacher.

That seems so long ago. And he was with his mother. Now he will have to go to the new school all by himself.

He does not like this one bit.

He rolls back and forth across the driveway, waiting for his parents to come outside. They both want to walk to school with him because it is the first day.

"Mom," he calls finally. "My stomach hurts. Maybe I should stay home."

He thinks about staying in his nice room, with his mom or dad reading books to him. Sometimes they do that when he's sick.

Bulldozer moves rocks around in the yard while he waits. He makes a big pile in front of the door. Soon he won't be able to see or hear his mother or father at all.

Bulldozer's father tries to come outside, but the pile of rocks is blocking the door.

"Now, B," he says. "Please clear these out of the way so your mother and I can open the door. You don't want to miss your first day of school."

That is exactly what Bulldozer *does* want...but he moves the rocks anyway and scoops up his backpack.

"I don't feel well," he says.

His mother comes outside with his lunch box and puts her hand on his cab. "You probably just have butterflies in your stomach, sweetie," she says.

Bulldozer wishes he *did* have butterflies in his stomach. That sounds kind of fun.

"I think I might really be sick," he warns them.

"Well, let's head to school and see how you feel when we get there," his mother says.

His father leads the way. "Come on, buddy. We don't want to be late."

Bulldozer rumbles along Diggity Drive, as slowly as possible, wishing he could turn around.

But his mom and dad don't seem to care. They are smiling and walking near him.

"This is exciting!" his father says. "Your first day at the new school! I'll have to take your picture when we get there."

Bulldozer wishes he could run out of gas on the way to school.

CHAPTER 2

Too Many People

Even though Bulldozer is going as slowly as possible, they are almost at the school. They pass the library and the little grocery store and the town park, and then there is only the big red building up ahead. It is much bigger than his old school.

All around it are people. So many people! Most of them are children.

Some are coming off the big yellow buses in front of the school. Some are walking with their mothers or fathers, like Bulldozer. Some are getting out of cars.

They have backpacks and lunch boxes.
They are laughing and talking.

Bulldozer has never seen so many new people before.

He stops his engine.

His mother and father turn around.

"What's up, B?" his father asks.

"It's too many people," Bulldozer says. "There's no room for me."

His mother pats him and puts his lunch box on his blade. "It's okay," she says. "We'll take you right to the door."

"I might run over someone," Bulldozer warns darkly.

"No, you won't, B. You're always careful about that," his father says.

Bulldozer is just trying to think of another reason he can't go to school when he hears a voice calling his name.

"B! B! Wait for me!"

It's Millie, the girl who lives across from his house on Diggity Drive. She is with her mother, Mrs. Patel, and her little brother, Jay.

Bulldozer is happy to see her. At least this is one person he knows.

"Hi," he says, feeling a little shy.

"Hi," says Millie. "We can go inside together."

Jay yells excitedly when he sees Bulldozer. "Truck, give me a ride! Give me a ride!" he says.

"Not today," Mrs. Patel says. "We don't want to make Millie and B late for school."

"I want to go to school!" Jay cries as his mom puts him down.

He tries to climb onto Bulldozer's blade.

"No, Jay," Mrs. Patel says, picking him up again. Jay leans out of her arms, reaching for Bulldozer.

"Me too!" he screams.

"Time for us to head home," Mrs. Patel says.

Bulldozer wishes he could trade places with Jay.

But at least he has Millie. He starts up his engine again and follows her toward the big front door of the school.

Their parents wave goodbye from the sidewalk.

"Have a great day!" his father shouts.

"We can't wait to hear all about it," his mother calls.

Bulldozer is too worried about school to answer them.

There are people everywhere. Millie stays close by his side. Some of the other kids are staring at them. Bulldozer does not like this. He wants to hide, but he is too big.

A man asks if they know where their classroom is.

"Room six," Millie says softly.

"Mrs. Bremmer."

"That's my teacher," says a boy with red hair.

"Great," the man says, smiling. He points. "You can go together. It's all the way down at the end."

The hallway is very long. It is full of kids.

The boy with red hair looks at Bulldozer. "Hey," he says. "Can you give us a ride?"

Bulldozer does not want this new boy, this boy he does not know, to climb on him.

But Millie grabs his door handle. "Is it okay?" she asks. "It'll be much faster."

Bulldozer does not want to say yes. But he also does not want to say no to Millie.

"I guess," he says.

"Yay!" says the boy with red hair. "I'm Ryan." He puts his foot on Bulldozer's tire and climbs onto his back.

Millie climbs up behind him. "I'm Millie," she says. "And this is B."

Bulldozer starts down the hallway.

"Look at us!" Ryan shouts. "Here we come!"

The other kids move to the side, and Bulldozer goes fast.

Soon they reach the door of room six.

A tall lady with curly black hair is waiting there.

"Hello!" she says. "I remember you three from the summer visit. Let's see…B, right? And Millie, and…"

"Ryan!" Ryan shouts.

"Good," says Mrs. Bremmer. "Come inside and meet your new friends. We will do so many fun things today."

The classroom is loud and busy. Bulldozer still feels scared. He is sure that nothing here is as fun as being home.

But Millie and Ryan are already sliding off his back and running inside, so what choice does he have?

Slowly, Bulldozer rolls into room six.

CHAPTER 3

Trouble at Circle Time

Some of the kids are sitting at tables. Some are standing by the windows. Some are playing with toys on the rug.

The toys are wooden blocks, colorful letters, and farm animals. Millie picks up a sheep.

Bulldozer wants to play, too. He rolls onto the rug. Millie starts to give him a toy horse, but before she can, Mrs. Bremmer claps her hands.

"Good morning, class," she says, smiling. "I think all our friends are here now."

Bulldozer doesn't know why she says that. These kids are not his friends. Only Millie is his friend.

"Can you put your backpack and lunch box in your cubby?" she asks. "You will see your name on it. If you have trouble finding it, I'll help you."

Bulldozer sees that there is a group of wooden boxes against the wall, next to a low bookcase. Each box has a name in red letters across the top.

He rolls over to put his lunch box in the cubby marked *B*. Millie comes with him.

"Look," she says. "Yours is right below mine."

That's good. That means his school stuff will be near Millie's.

But just as Bulldozer is lifting his blade to place his lunch box inside his cubby, he bangs the corner of the bookcase, hard.

It wobbles.

Oh no!

The whole bookcase tips over. Books spill onto the floor.

Bulldozer freezes. The other kids stare. Then they start laughing.

"Sorry," Bulldozer says. He feels bad.

"That's okay, B," Mrs. Bremmer says.

"Accidents happen. Who would like to help put the books back?"

She stands the bookcase up, and Millie helps her with the books.

"Thank you, Millie," Mrs. Bremmer says. "Now, class, let's clean up the toys. Then we'll sit on the rug for Circle Time."

Bulldozer is nervous about Circle Time. The toys are everywhere. Cleaning up goes very slowly.

Bulldozer has an idea. Moving things is what he does best! He lowers his blade.

"Watch out," he tells the kids as he pushes all the toys off the rug, into a pile.

He waits for the teacher to say what a big help he is.

But Mrs. Bremmer looks surprised.

"Oh my goodness," she says. "Children, can you help B put the toys in the right bins?"

Now Bulldozer feels worse. He was only trying to help. And besides, it is a waste of time to put the toys in different bins. They will just get mixed up again.

Ryan runs over to him. "Wow, you did that so fast!"

That makes Bulldozer feel a tiny bit better.

All the kids sit down on the rug.

"Crisscross applesauce," Mrs. Bremmer tells them, and they sit with crossed legs.

Bulldozer can't sit that way.

He is beginning to think that school is a place he just doesn't belong.

Oh, how he wishes he were home!

"Now we will have Circle Time," Mrs. Bremmer says. "We will each share something special with the class. Who would like to go first?"

Nobody wants to go first, so Mrs. Bremmer says that she went to the beach on Saturday and saw a starfish. She holds up a picture for everyone to see. The starfish is white with five points, just like a star. Bulldozer thinks it is very pretty.

Then other kids start telling about stuff they found at the beach. Somebody found goose poop. Everybody thinks that's funny.

Mrs. Bremmer says, "Ryan, do you have something you would like to share that isn't about the beach?"

Ryan says he found a quarter on the way to school. He digs it out of his pocket and shows the class. The quarter is round and silver and shiny. Everybody thinks Ryan is very lucky.

Bulldozer feels even more nervous. What is he going to talk about?

Now it's Millie's turn. She tells the story of saving the orange cat that was stuck in the tree.

Wait! That was Bulldozer's story. He was the one who saved Sunset. Now he can't talk about that.

A boy named Peter says he can bend his thumb all the way down to touch his arm, and then he shows everyone.

Bulldozer is getting more and more worried.

Then the teacher calls on him.

"What about you, B? What would you like to share with the class?" Mrs. Bremmer asks.

Bulldozer can't think of anything.

"Hey," Ryan says. "Do something cool."

"Yeah," Millie adds. "Show us one of your tricks, B."

Tricks? What tricks?

Bulldozer tries to think.

"I can back up and beep at the same time," he says. "Watch."

He starts backing up, with a loud BEEP-BEEP-BEEP warning sound.

"Wow!" "Cool!" the other kids shout.

But Bulldozer can't see where he's going, and suddenly there's a loud CRUNCH.

"Stop!" Mrs. Bremmer cries.

CHAPTER 4

The Playground

It is too late. Behind Bulldozer is a table…or what used to be a table. Now it's all bent and crushed.

"Hey," says a girl named Katie. "That's my table. You smashed it!"

She starts to cry.

The three other kids who sat at the table with Katie start crying, too.

Bulldozer cannot believe this is happening. First he knocked over the bookcase. Then he messed up the toys. Then he ran over a table.

This is the worst day of his life! And it is only the first day of school. He's never coming back here again.

"Oh dear," Mrs. Bremmer says. She covers her mouth with her hand. Bulldozer is afraid she is about to yell at him.

"I didn't mean to," he says softly.

"I know you didn't," Mrs. Bremmer says. "It's important to always look where you're going. Right, everyone?"

She stands for a minute, looking at the smashed table. "Well, what's done is done," she says. "Don't worry, we will get another table. It's time for lunch, and then recess. Let's line up at the door."

Bulldozer lines up behind Millie. "It was just an accident," she whispers to him. "It's okay."

But there is nothing okay about this, Bulldozer knows.

The lunchroom is very noisy, and there are too many kids. But Bulldozer sits with Millie and Ryan, and nothing bad happens, thank goodness.

After lunch, it's time to go outside.

Bulldozer rolls down the hallway, following the line of kids to the door that leads to the playground.

Outside, the sun is shining and there are kids everywhere. Some are sitting on the swings or going down the slide. Some are climbing up ladders or hanging from monkey bars. Some are playing in the sandbox.

Millie and Ryan stand with Bulldozer, looking at the busy playground.

"There's no room for us," Ryan says glumly.

It's true. All the swings are taken. There's a long line for the slide.

"Let's play over there," Millie says, pointing to the grass. "We can make up our own game."

What will they play? Bulldozer rolls behind Millie and Ryan as they walk to the other side of the playground.

"There's nothing here," Ryan says.

Bulldozer looks around. At the edge of the grass, near the woods, he sees a big rock.

"I know," he says. "Let's build a clubhouse."

Millie smiles. "That's a great idea!"

"Yeah!" Ryan shouts.

"I'll get that rock," Bulldozer says.

"That giant rock?" Millie asks. "It will be too heavy."

"I can do it," Bulldozer tells her. "Can you and Ryan make a fence out of sticks?"

"Sure," says Millie. "There are lots of sticks on the ground."

Bulldozer rumbles over to the big rock. It is almost as tall as his engine. He lowers his blade and pushes it.

Oof! It's heavy.

But it moves! Some of the grass comes with it, but Bulldozer doesn't think anyone will notice.

He pushes the rock over to where Millie and Ryan are building a fence out of sticks.

"Wow," Ryan says. "Our clubhouse has a big rock wall. It's like a *castle*."

That makes Bulldozer feel good. He is building a castle! A castle is even better than a clubhouse.

One of the recess teachers calls out, "What are you kids doing over there?"

Uh-oh. Now the teacher will ruin their fun.

"We're just building something," Millie says sweetly.

"Huh." The teacher squints at them. "Where did that big rock come from?"

"It's not a rock, it's a CASTLE!" Ryan shouts.

Katie, the girl whose table got smashed, comes over. "What are you doing?" she asks.

"We're making a castle," Bulldozer tells her.

"Can I help?" she asks.

"Sure," Millie says.

Millie, Ryan, and Katie keep picking up sticks and building the fence.

In no time, more kids come over. It turns out everybody wants to build the castle.

"How did you move that big rock?" a boy named Luke asks.

Millie and Ryan point to Bulldozer.

"We couldn't have done it without B!" Millie says.

Bulldozer is filled with pride. He lifts his blade to stand even taller.

"Wow, you must be really strong," Luke says.

"I am." Bulldozer tries not to brag. He wants Luke to like him, and he knows that it is hard to like people who brag.

While the kids finish the fence, Bulldozer pushes up a wall of dirt around the castle.

With everybody helping, the castle is almost finished.

"We need something to sit on inside," Katie says.

Bulldozer finds a log near the woods and carries it to the castle on his blade.

"That's perfect, B," Millie says.

Bump! Bulldozer drops the log.

The kids roll it next to the rock to make a bench.

"That will be a nice place to sit." Katie smiles at Bulldozer. Maybe she has forgotten about her smashed table.

"We just need something for the door," Millie says.

They all look around. They need something big enough to block the gap in the fence but not too heavy for them to swing open and shut.

Hmmm.

"I know!" says Luke. "Look over there! Cardboard."

At the edge of the playground, there is a giant blue dumpster. Next to it is a big piece of cardboard.

"Let's go get it," Luke says to Bulldozer, and he climbs up onto his back.

Bulldozer is surprised, but he thinks the cardboard will make a good door, so he rolls across the playground to the dumpster. Luke reaches down and grabs the cardboard.

"Children!" the recess teacher yells.
"Stay away from that garbage."

Quickly, they zoom back to the castle.

Luke puts the cardboard across the opening and shows everyone how he can slide it back and forth. It's a door that opens and closes!

"This is the best castle EVER," Ryan says.

And it is. It really is.

Just then the bell rings.

Recess is over.

"Line up, class!" Mrs. Bremmer calls.

Ugh. Bulldozer does not want to go back inside the classroom. Inside is where the trouble is.

But he feels happy about the castle.

Millie walks next to him in line and holds on to his door handle.

"We made something new, B!" she says happily. "All because of you."

CHAPTER 5
Cleaning Up

As soon as they are back in the classroom, Bulldozer starts to worry. What if he makes another mistake? What if he crashes into something else? He tries hard to stay in one place, but sometimes he wants to move around.

He tells himself he only has to be careful until three o'clock. That's when school is over. Then he will get to go home. He can't wait.

To his surprise, the rest of the day is not that bad. Mrs. Bremmer reads the class a story about Paul Bunyan. He is *big*, like Bulldozer!

Next they do spelling, and Bulldozer is good at spelling. Then Mrs. Bremmer gives them each a blank piece of paper.

"Draw your favorite thing about school so far," she tells them.

Bulldozer can't draw very well, so Millie helps him.

"What do you want to draw?" Millie asks.

Bulldozer thinks for a minute. "The castle," he says.

"That's what I drew!" Millie says.

"Me too!" Ryan yells.

"Me too!" say Katie and Peter.

Mrs. Bremmer is walking around the room, looking at the pictures. "Is that a house?" she asks Millie.

"Kind of," Millie says. "We made a castle on the playground."

Then everyone wants to tell Mrs. Bremmer about the castle.

"It looks amazing," Mrs. Bremmer says. "Where did the big rock come from?"

"B found it!" the children shout.

And Mrs. Bremmer smiles at Bulldozer. "It looks like you made the first day of school special for everyone, B," she says.

And Bulldozer is so happy he can't think of anything to say.

Soon the day is almost over. Mrs. Bremmer claps her hands. "Okay, class, cleanup time. Please put the trash from your snacks in the garbage bag. And let's pick up the toys that are on the rug."

Everyone helps clean up the classroom. It goes quickly because they are all working together.

"What good helpers!" Mrs. Bremmer says. "I'll take the trash out to the hallway."

She is just lifting the big garbage bag when the bag *breaks*.

Trash spills all over the floor… dirty napkins, juice boxes, crackers and pretzels and carrot sticks.

"Oh no," Mrs. Bremmer says. "What a mess."

Bulldozer knows just what to do. He rolls over to the pile. "I can clean it up," he tells her.

"Oh, can you, B?" Mrs. Bremmer says. "That would be wonderful."

She shows Bulldozer where to put the trash, and he lowers his blade and pushes the pile into the hallway. Then he scoops it up and drops it in the big trash bin.

"Good job, B!" Mrs. Bremmer says. "All right, everyone, let's make a line for buses and pickup."

She gives the class a big smile. "I loved spending the day with all of you. I can't wait for us to be together tomorrow."

Bulldozer does not feel that way, but he thinks it's a nice thing for Mrs. Bremmer to say. And he decides school is not so bad. It is not great, but it's okay.

The class lines up and walks down the hall. Bulldozer, Millie, and Ryan are all getting picked up, so they go to the cafeteria. Bulldozer's parents are there waiting for him.

"Hi, B! How was your first day?" his mother asks. "Did you have fun?"

"We want to hear all about it," his father says.

Bulldozer tells them everything that happened: how he made a mess with the toys on the rug, knocked over the bookcase, and crushed the table. But also how he built a castle! And how he cleaned up the trash when the bag broke.

"Oh my goodness, that is quite a day," his mother says.

"It sounds like you did just fine," his father says. "And you made a castle! I want to see that."

"Bye, B!" Millie calls.

"Yeah, bye!" Ryan yells.

"Wait a second," his father says. "I forgot to take a picture this morning—can I take one with your new friends?"

"Sure," Bulldozer says.

Millie stands next to him and holds his door handle. Ryan climbs up on his front tire.

"Ready?" Bulldozer's father takes their picture.

His mother smiles at them. "Look at you three! Starting a new school year."

Bulldozer feels happy…because he went to school!

And because now he gets to go home.

Turn the page to try some fun activities with Bulldozer and his friends. . . .

Word Play

Now get your own piece of paper and a pencil (please don't write in this book). Bulldozer, Millie, Ryan, and Mrs. Bremmer need your help. Let's see what they want you to do.

Bulldozer wants to:

1. MAKE A PILE OF ADJECTIVES

An adjective is a word that **describes** a person, place, or thing.

Here are three adjectives from *Bulldozer Goes to School*:

tall   **red**   **strong**

Can you help Bulldozer find five more? Write them on your paper.

Wow! You were a big help! Now can you help Millie?

2. DIG UP SOME WORDS THAT END IN -ING

Millie wants to find action words ending in **-ing.**

Here are three from chapter 1:

reading   **smiling**   **walking**

Can you help Millie dig up five more words that end in **-ing** in chapter 2? Write them on your paper.

Good job! But now guess who needs your help? More kids from Millie and B's class.

3. RACE TO THE PLAYGROUND WORDS

Ryan and Katie want to collect some words related to a playground. Here are three from the book:

kids **slide** **fence**

Can you help Ryan and Katie find five more in chapter 4? Write them on your paper.

That's great! Now there's just one last thing. Bulldozer's teacher, Mrs. Bremmer, needs your help, too. Do you think you can help a grown-up?

4. SHOVEL UP WORDS THAT MEAN FEELINGS

Mrs. Bremmer wants you to find words that describe how someone **feels**. The very first line of this book is:

Bulldozer is nervous.

The word **nervous** describes how B feels about the first day of school.

Can you look through the book and help Mrs. Bremmer find five more words that describe how someone feels? Write them on your paper.

YAY! YOU DID IT!

Bulldozer, Millie, Ryan, Katie, and Mrs. Bremmer say thank you—and they wish you could be in their class, too!

Elise Broach

is the *New York Times* bestselling author of nearly thirty books for children, including *Bulldozer's Big Rescue*, the first book in the Bulldozer and Friends chapter book series; the acclaimed Masterpiece Adventures chapter book series; picture books such as *Bedtime for Little Bulldozer* and *When Dinosaurs Came with Everything*; and the mysteries *Duet, Masterpiece, Shakespeare's Secret, The Wolf Keepers*, and the Superstition Mountain trilogy. She lives in Connecticut. Elise invites you to visit her at elisebroach.com.

Kelly Murphy

has illustrated many popular books for children, including *Bulldozer's Big Rescue*, the Masterpiece Adventures series, and *Masterpiece*, as well as *Faraway Things* by Dave Eggers. She lives in Providence, Rhode Island, and invites you to visit her at kelmurphy.com.

This book is a work of fiction. Names, characters, places, and incidents are the product of the author's imagination or are used fictitiously. Any resemblance to actual events, locales, or persons, living or dead, is coincidental.

Text copyright © 2025 by Elise Broach
Illustrations copyright © 2025 by Kelly Murphy

Cover art copyright © 2025 by Kelly Murphy. Cover design by Patrick Hulse.
Cover copyright © 2025 by Hachette Book Group, Inc.
Interior design by Carla Weise.

Hachette Book Group supports the right to free expression and the value of copyright. The purpose of copyright is to encourage writers and artists to produce the creative works that enrich our culture.

The scanning, uploading, and distribution of this book without permission is a theft of the author's intellectual property. If you would like permission to use material from the book (other than for review purposes), please contact permissions@hbgusa.com. Thank you for your support of the author's rights.

Christy Ottaviano Books
Hachette Book Group
1290 Avenue of the Americas, New York, NY 10104
Visit us at LBYR.com

First Edition: July 2025

Christy Ottaviano Books is an imprint of Little, Brown and Company.
The Christy Ottaviano Books name and logo are registered trademarks
of Hachette Book Group, Inc.

The publisher is not responsible for websites (or their content)
that are not owned by the publisher.

Little, Brown and Company books may be purchased in bulk for business, educational, or promotional use. For information, please contact your local bookseller or the Hachette Book Group Special Markets Department at special.markets@hbgusa.com.

Library of Congress Cataloging-in-Publication Data
Names: Broach, Elise, author. | Murphy, Kelly, illustrator.
Title: Bulldozer goes to school / Elise Broach ; illustrated by Kelly Murphy.
Description: First edition. | New York : Little, Brown and Company, 2025. | Series: Bulldozer and friends ; 2 | "Christy Ottaviano Books." | Audience: Ages 6–9. | Summary: Bulldozer is nervous about his first day of school, but at the end of the day he decides it is not so bad.
Identifiers: LCCN 2024038481 | ISBN 9780316564205 (paperback) | ISBN 9780316564199 (hardcover) | ISBN 9780316564212 (ebook)
Subjects: CYAC: Bulldozers—Fiction. | First day of school—Fiction. | Schools—Fiction.
Classification: LCC PZ7.B78083 Bs 2025 | DDC [Fic]—dc23
LC record available at https://lccn.loc.gov/2024038481

ISBNs: 978-0-316-56419-9 (hardcover), 978-0-316-56420-5 (paperback), 978-0-316-56421-2 (ebook)

PRINTED IN DONGGUAN, CHINA

APS

Hardcover: 10 9 8 7 6 5 4 3 2 1
Paperback: 10 9 8 7 6 5 4 3 2 1